D0674340

Might goes hand in hand with right as He-Man and the Masters of the Universe fight to make their planet safe. The greatest of their enemies is Skeletor, the Lord of Destruction, and his evil band, whose hatred for their foes is never-ending. The war goes on but who will win?

First edition

© LADYBIRD BOOKS LTD MCMLXXXIV and MATTEL INC MCMLXXXIV

MASTERS
OF THE UNIVERSE™

Skeletor's Ice Attack

by John Grant
illustrated by Robin Davies

Ladybird Books Loughborough

It was a bright, sunny day in the port of
Randorhaven. Flags waved in the sea breeze,
and crowds lined the quayside to cheer as King
Randor and Queen Marlena prepared to embark
in the royal ship, *Sea Eagle*. Their son Prince
Adam was with them, and also his childhood
friend, Teela. The royal family stepped into the
royal hover-barge and were swiftly ferried across
the harbour. With a beating of drums and
fanfares of trumpets they went aboard *Sea*

4

Eagle. The King and Queen and even Teela greeted the captain with proper dignity. But King Randor frowned at Prince Adam who was too excited at the thought of the summer holiday in the Golden Isles. He laughed and shouted, and waved to the sailors and the crowd on shore, who waved and shouted back. No one suspected that the happy-go-lucky prince was also He-Man, mightiest man in the Universe.

The decks of *Sea Eagle* bustled with activity as the crew prepared for sea. Baggage was taken below. The passengers were shown to their cabins. The royal hover-barge returned to shore.

No one noticed a sinister shape lurking in the shadows close to the hull of *Sea Eagle*. It was part-human, but covered in scales; one of the Sea-People, a servant of Mer-Man, Lord of the Sea.

His head above water, the evil creature strained his ears as the crew spoke amongst themselves.

"Looks like being a good voyage."

"Yes. I always enjoy the trip to the Golden Isles."

"I hope the weather stays calm for His Majesty and family."

"Right. Now let's get this gear stowed. We sail with the tide."

Even before *Sea Eagle* had weighed anchor, or before the officers on the bridge had set the electronic sail controls, the spy was already speeding under water towards the caverns of the Sea-People.

Far below the surface, Mer-Man sat in the dim green light of his underwater lair. He wanted power. But to gain power he needed to find favour with his master, Skeletor, Lord of Destruction. Suddenly there was a commotion outside. Two guards came in, escorting a

panting sea-creature. He threw himself at Mer-Man's feet.

"Master!" he gasped. "Your enemies have set sail in a ship. Their course is towards the Golden Isles!"

Mer-Man jumped to his feet. "Alone on the sea. They are at my mercy. This must be reported to My Lord Skeletor immediately."

Within seconds, word came back from the Lord of Destruction. "Capture the royal family of Eternia and hold them to ransom. And this time, don't bungle it in your usual way!"

Quickly Mer-Man issued his orders. Then, on
a giant monitor screen he watched as the *Sea
Eagle* sped across the surface of the sea, the hull
just above the waves. Mer-Man pointed to a
chart carved on the rock wall of the cavern. "By
nightfall, the ship will have reached this point.
That is where I shall set my trap."

Through the slimy caverns and passages of the
undersea world the Sea-People hurried to the
assembly point. Each was armed with a zero-
energy projector.

At a command from Mer-Man the outer gates of his fortress were thrown open. In a shimmering column of scaly bodies his people glided swiftly through the green depths to intercept *Sea Eagle* and her royal passengers.

The sun had set below the horizon when Mer-Man halted his people. Rising carefully just above the water he scanned the surface of the sea. In the last of the light he could just make out the gleam of sails as the royal ship sailed straight into Mer-Man's trap.

On board, King Randor and Prince Adam
had joined the captain on the bridge. All was
quiet. Lights flickered on the navigation panel.
The wheel was on automatic pilot. Only
occasionally an officer adjusted the sail controls
as the wind changed slightly. The King and his
son went to their cabins, and the great ship flew
across the waves and into the gathering
darkness.

Mer-Man took one last look. Then he gave the command. The Sea-People spread out into a wide circle, and as the *Sea Eagle* reached the centre they aimed their weapons and fired.

As the zero-energy was released the sea began to freeze. A thin film of ice formed around the ship. It grew thicker. It formed into hummocks and pinnacles. Soon, the *Sea Eagle* was trapped in the middle of a giant ice-floe. Mer-Man dismissed his people, then waited to decide his next move.

On the bridge of *Sea Eagle* the instruments showed the speed of the ship rapidly dropping. The captain ordered powerful searchlights to be switched on. At first there was nothing to see. Then one of the sailors cried out, "Captain, look at the sea! There's something happening to it!" The waves had stopped moving. "The sea is freezing," cried the captain. "We must break out. Set more sail." But even as the controls were adjusted the ice was growing thicker, and piling up around the ship.

Sea Eagle was trapped and helpless. The passengers and crew dressed in cold-weather gear and examined the ice from the deck.

"We must try to blast our way out," said the captain. The ship's weapons were trained on the ice, but even after several minutes firing, they had no effect. When dawn came, the ship was held as firmly as before.

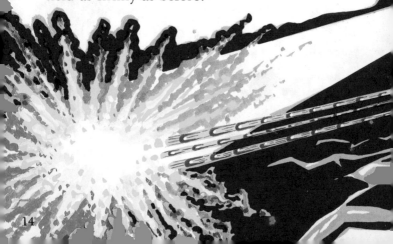

In his cabin, Prince Adam was thinking about the situation. "This is the work of Skeletor, or one of his evil band," he said to himself. "It is time for the Masters of the Universe to take a hand." He pulled the Sword of Power from its hiding place among his clothes in a chest. Unsheathing the Sword he cried:

"BY THE POWER OF GRAYSKULL!"

... and was instantly transformed into He-Man.

Using the power of the blade he sent out a powerful tele-summons to Man-at-Arms back at Castle Grayskull to join him secretly in Talon Fighter. Then he made his way stealthily to the ship's chart room. There, after a quick search, he found the chart he was looking for. Then he hurried back to his cabin to study it and complete his plans.

With the chart spread on the cabin table, He-Man worked out the position of *Sea Eagle*. Then he thought, "While the ship is trapped in the ice we may be attacked at any time. There is only one way to melt an ice-floe of this size. We must try to harness the power of Inferno Island. It is a long way off. But it is our only chance."

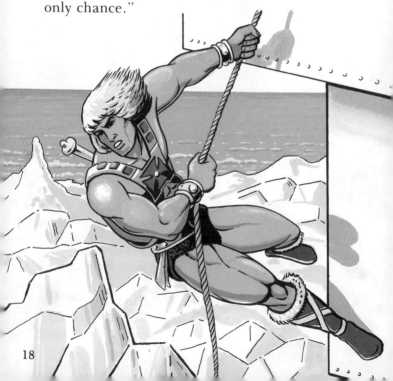

Rolling up the chart and tucking it into his belt He-Man slipped out of the cabin and up on deck. It was deserted as the passengers and crew stayed below decks out of the bitter cold from the ice. Taking a coil of rope, He-Man tied it to the ship's rail and climbed down it.

The ice was piled in a great jumbled mass. After a few steps He-Man was out of sight of the ship. But he hurried on until he came to the water's edge where the floe was flat and smooth. Even as he did so the Sword of Power began to pulsate with light as it picked up a homing signal from Talon Fighter.

Hidden among the ice hummocks He-Man watched for the first sign of Talon Fighter. From far off he made out the roar of the craft's jets. Then the sound stopped as Man-at-Arms cut the power and swooped down in a fast, silent glide, close above the waves and hidden from the *Sea Eagle* by the ice. One quick burst of reverse thrust and the sleek craft was down and sliding to a halt close to He-Man.

Man-at-Arms stepped out of the cockpit and grasped He-Man by the hand. "I think that this mischief is the work of that green trouble-maker Mer-Man. I saw a lot of activity below the waves as I flew over."

He-Man showed Man-at-Arms the chart. "I don't know exactly what Mer-Man is likely to be plotting," he said. "But we have not a moment to lose."

With He-Man at the controls, Talon Fighter lifted from the ice and in a moment was a shining speck against the sky.

With its controls locked on to the course already worked out by He-Man from the borrowed chart, Talon Fighter flashed through the sky. Soon the ice-floe and the imprisoned *Sea Eagle* were left far behind. He-Man strained his eyes, scanning the horizon. Then he cried out, "There it is! Dead ahead! Inferno Island!"

Soon they could make out clearly the smoking top of the island. The smoke rose in a column higher even than Talon Fighter, and He-Man took over the controls and made a wide circle to avoid it.

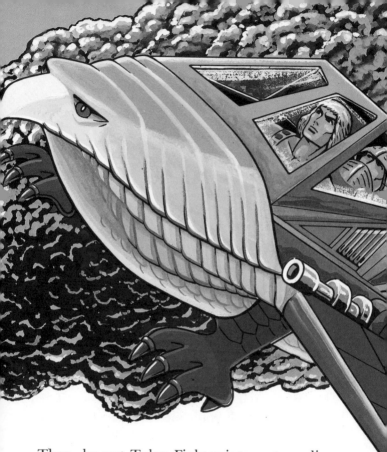

Then, he put Talon Fighter into a steep dive
that brought them close to the crater of the
volcano. The craft bounced and buffeted in the
hot air currents rising from the fiery island. It
took all of He-Man's mighty strength to hold a
steady course round the rim of the crater where
molten lava bubbled and fumed close to
overflowing.

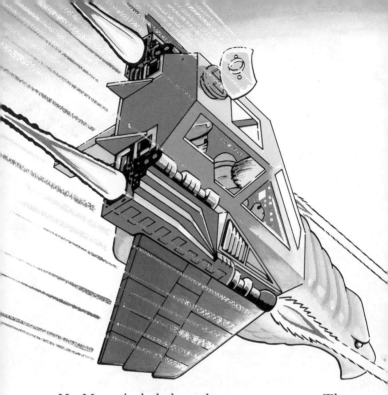

He-Man circled the volcano once more. Then
he swung Talon Fighter into position for a long,
fast dive towards the crater's rim. Jets screaming
at full power, Talon Fighter hurtled downwards.
Then He-Man pressed the firing controls on the
laser cannons. White-hot streaks of energy leapt
from the muzzles, and fragments of rock flew
into the air. The rim of the crater crumbled
and collapsed. As He-Man pulled his craft up
and away in a tight turn the whole side of the
volcano collapsed. Molten lava rolled in a

burning river across the island. When it reached
the sea the water boiled with great clouds of
steam. Swiftly the boiling water moved out from
the island. A current of the steaming water was
already travelling in the direction of the *Sea
Eagle*. Once there, it would melt the ice and the
ship would be free.

Racing ahead of the current, Talon Fighter
drew close to the ice-floe. As Man-at-Arms had
done, He-Man came in low. And through the
clear water he saw the Sea-People massing for
the attack. The warm current was going to
arrive too late!

He-Man brought Talon Fighter in to hover just above the ice. Then he jumped out, while Man-at-Arms again took to the air. His job was to keep watch on the activities of the Sea-People.

Boarding the ship in the same way as he had left it, He-Man hurried to find Teela and explained what he and Man-at-Arms had been doing. As the Warrior Goddess, her powers were almost equal to his own, and he wanted her help. "The warm sea current is moving too slowly," he explained. "We must go to meet it. While Mer-man has at his command great numbers of the creatures of the sea, there are many of whom he is not master. The warm-blooded sea-dwellers count him as their enemy. Perhaps they will come to our aid. Will you try?"

"Yes," replied Teela. "If I can reach enough of them by thought-energy they will do as I ask."

Following He-Man,
Teela climbed down on
to the ice. They looked for
a high place, and found an
ice pinnacle. He-Man helped
Teela to stand on top of it.
Then she raised her Kobra
sceptre above her head. As her
thought-energy flowed into
it the eyes began to pulse
with power.

Soon the eyes of the sceptre glowed steadily and brightly. Teela closed her eyes and began to transmit a silent message by the power of her mind.

"I, TEELA, WARRIOR GODDESS, SUMMON YOU WHO HAVE WARM BLOOD, BY COMMAND OF THE LORD HE-MAN."

He-Man scanned the waves. But nothing moved. Again Teela sent out her message. And again.

Then, far off, there appeared a puff of
vapour above the waves. Then another. And
another. A school of whales was approaching.
A herd of walruses suddenly surfaced close to the
ice. Dolphins came leaping over the crests of the
waves. And a school of porpoises followed quickly.
More and more whales, walruses, dolphins,
porpoises and a huge herd of seals joined them.
In her mind Teela heard their thoughts:

"COMMAND US, TEELA. WE ARE HERE
TO DO YOUR BIDDING."

He-Man looked at the sea animals as they jostled beside the ice-floe.

"Now," he said to Teela, "command them to push against the ice."

Again Teela raised the Kobra sceptre, and again the eyes glowed as she sent out more mind energy:

"USE YOUR STRENGTH. PUSH AGAINST THE ICE."

With a great threshing of tails, fins and flippers the whales, walruses, dolphins, porpoises and seals pushed hard. At first nothing happened. Then slowly the great ice-floe began to move. It gathered speed, heading steadily for the warm current flowing from Inferno Island.

Again, He-Man scanned the surface of the sea for any sign of Mer-Man. But the Sea-People were keeping out of sight because Man-at-Arms was circling above. There was nothing more that He-Man and Teela could do for the moment. He-Man said, "You go back to the ship. I will get Man-at-Arms to pick me up."

He waited until she had gone, then changed into Prince Adam once more and made his way, unseen, back to the ship as well.

Far away in his lair in Snake Mountain Skeletor, Lord of Destruction, was uneasy. He decided to spy on his underlings, and activated his spy-scan monitor. All seemed well. Then, he tuned in to Mer-Man.

At first it looked as though Mer-Man was winning the day. On the screen *Sea Eagle* appeared trapped in the ice. Below the surface of the sea was Mer-Man, surrounded by his warriors.

But when Skeletor looked again, he saw that the ice-floe in which *Sea Eagle* was trapped

was itself moving – *away* from the undersea army!

Skeletor screamed with rage, and his slaves fled in terror. "That fool!" he roared. "His bungling will bring disaster to us all."

Shouting an order to his scurrying slaves, he raced out to his fast and deadly hovercraft. His Roton was ready for him, prepared for take-off. Scattering the ground crew before him, Skeletor leapt aboard, and a moment later was flashing across the coast and out to sea.

From a distance Skeletor spotted the trapped *Sea Eagle*. As he got closer he saw the great mass of creatures pushing the ice-floe. Desperate to know what was happening, Skeletor called up Mer-Man.

Mer-Man's face appeared on the cockpit video screen.

"You spineless jelly-fish!" Skeletor shrieked. "This is some trick of the Masters of the Universe! Do something about it!"

"I'll order my warriors..." stammered Mer-Man.

"Warriors? Witless sea-urchins!" cried
Skeletor. "Summon the sharks, sting rays, sea-
serpents to attack those interfering
air-breathers!"

Mer-Man did as he was ordered, climbing on
to the ice to direct operations.

Skeletor watched with satisfaction as a swarm
of sharks, sting rays and sea-serpents raced to
the attack. Then he guided the Roton in to
alight on the ice. He still had to deal with Mer-
Man.

As the Roton skidded to a standstill Skeletor leapt out and climbed on to an ice hummock. He saw Mer-Man standing on another hummock. And he also saw the sharks, sting rays and sea-serpents fleeing for their lives.

A school of highly intelligent killer whales had been patrolling at the rear of Teela's creatures as they pushed the ice-floe. Now they rushed to the attack, teeth gleaming, quickly joined by the long-tusked walruses.

Mer-Man shouted after them in rage.
"Cowards! Come back!" And he fired shots from
his energy weapon into the waves, but could not
stop the retreat.

Beside himself with rage, Skeletor aimed a
shot at Mer-Man. But it went wide as his foot
slipped. The ice was melting. The floe was
breaking up.

Mer-Man fired blasts of ice pellets, and so the
two evil creatures battled it out on the wet,
slippery ice, ducking and dodging among the
crumbling hummocks.

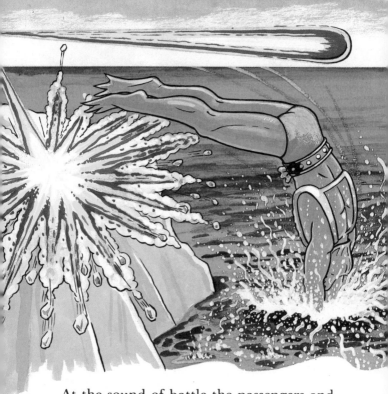

At the sound of battle the passengers and crew of *Sea Eagle* rushed on deck. Already they could feel the air becoming milder as the ice melted.

They saw Mer-Man fire once again at Skeletor. Mer-Man slipped on the ice. He sprawled full-length and his weapon flew from his hand. It slid along the ice and over the edge. Weaponless, Mer-Man decided to follow. In a hail of shots from Skeletor he dived into the water and disappeared.

Alone on the ice, Skeletor made to escape in the Roton. But he had left it too late. The ice-floe was already breaking into fragments. A wide lane of water separated him from his machine which drifted farther off even as he watched.

The ice under Skeletor's feet gave a lurch. The piece upon which he was standing had broken free of the main floe and was drifting off, carrying him with it.

Standing by the ship's rail, Prince Adam and Teela watched Skeletor's plight. "I feel almost sorry for him," said Teela.

Skeletor clung in terror to the rapidly shrinking piece of ice. "Mer-Man!" he screamed. "I command you to come to my aid! I am your lord and master!"

There was a swirl in the water. But it was not Mer-Man. One of the killer whales was in a playful mood. It swam close. Then it dived under Skeletor, making the ice rock violently.

Again Skeletor shouted for Mer-Man.

Adam turned to Teela. "Mer-Man is not the bravest of creatures," he said. "Skeletor is going to be very cold and wet before Mer-Man plucks up courage to face him, let alone rescue him."

The last piece of ice drifted clear of *Sea Eagle*. The captain shouted an order, and the sails filled to the freshening breeze. The great ship gathered way, faster and faster, until the wind sang in the rigging and she scarcely seemed to touch even the tops of the waves.

The passengers looked astern. Already far behind the last pieces of ice bobbed on the waves. On one the Roton could be seen. And on another the tiny figure of Skeletor waved and shouted for Mer-Man.

But Adam, with Teela by his side, was looking at the sky. Away in the distance, he could see a silvery streak against the blue. It was the Talon Fighter returning to Castle Grayskull with Man-at-Arms. The Masters of the Universe had triumphed once again.